AF400578

Christelle Angano

# The Flowers of the lake

elephantsetpattesdemouche.com

Christelle Angano is a French author.

Through her works, she enjoys taking her readers on a journey—not only through her beloved Normandy, but also to more distant lands. She also addresses social issues, on which she does not hesitate to take a stand. She places great importance on the work of remembrance and has dedicated a trilogy, The Clara Cycle, to her great-grandmother. Clara Matthews Chompton, a British-born woman who became a naturalised French citizen, was arrested following a denunciation and died in deportation for helping paratroopers from the British 9th Battalion during D-Day.

In 2022, she chose to leave the national education system to dedicate herself entirely to writing and founded her own business, Éléphants et pattes de mouches.

She now devotes herself fully to writing, leads workshops, and has also decided to expand her work as a ghostwriter.

Traduction par Amy Wells de *Les Fleurs du lac* (même auteure), publié aux Éditions de la Rémanence, février 2019

Mise en page par Amélie Quermont - Relectrice, Correctrice (www.ameliequermont.com)

Photo de couverture : propriété de Christelle Angano

# The Flowers of the lake

For Giulia<br>
For Géraldine<br>
For all of those who resist.

*"Anyone who excises a woman, regardless of age, shall be punished by imprisonment for a term of not less than three months or by a fine of not less than 500 Birr."*
Ethiopian Penal Code, Article 565


*"Whoever performs genital infibulation on a woman shall be punished by imprisonment with hard labour for a term of 3 to 5 years.*
*"For any injury caused to the body or health which is the result of the act described in the above paragraph, subject to the provisions of the Penal Code which provide for more severe penalties, the applicable penalty shall be a term of imprisonment of 5 to 10 years."*
Ethiopian Penal Code, Article 566

Across the world,
a little girl is excised every ten seconds.

# Preface

I wrote *Les Fleurs du lac* several years ago.

It was my way of shedding light on the women — and also the men —who dedicate all their energy to pushing back and eliminating a practice that seems to belong to another age : female genital mutilation (FGM).

I was asked for an English version. Here it is.

I chose to set my story in Ethiopia — a country where I lived for many years, a country that deeply moved me and that I loved profoundly. Through writing, I was able to rediscover the landscapes that had once charmed me, places that, even after all these years, still resonate within me. It made sense, to me, that my heroine should be Ethiopian. And my friends "from there" recognised that too — and for this, I thank them.

I dedicate this novel to all the Mebrat of the world — present and future.

I dedicate it to all the men who support these women in their quest and in their struggle.

To Fatoumata and Awa, two young Senegalese schoolgirls who wrote to tell me of their decision to join Mebrat in her fight.

To that young Djiboutian mother who wrote to say that, after reading my novel, she had decided not to sacrifice her second daughter to tradition.

I dedicate it to her little daughter.

I dedicate it to the young woman I met who had undergone FGM in France — yes, in France — thirty years ago.

I dedicate it to this woman, photographed over 40 years ago — upright, proud, strong, and so elegant. She inspired me the character of Mebrat.

And finally, more than ever, I dedicate it to my friend Nafissatu Fall, president of GAMS Normandie, whose commitment, courage, and determination never cease to impress me.

***

Mebrat is a real heroine. She's one of those women who knows how to say no, who knows how to fight. A courageous and strong woman... as women know how to be. Mebrat dares. Like Rosa

Parks, who refused to give up her seat, Malala, who was determined to go to school and almost died because of it, Simone Veil, who defended women so well, or Meaza Ashenafi, who worked tirelessly for the cause of her compatriots in Addis Ababa.

I wanted to write a positive novel that leaves room for hope, a tribute to all the women who have decided to take action. A militant novel, certainly ; but as a lawyer, never as a prosecutor.

Finally, I'd like to quote my friend Géraldine, who once said to me : "I'd get down on my knees to put an end to the excision of young girls."

This book will be my contribution.

*"When faced with excision, you have to say not me, not my sisters, not my cousins."*
Aminata

# It all started somewhere in Ethiopia, in the 1980s

# Eyes Mother

A bluish dawn was breaking gently over the lake. The friendly stars accompanied their accomplice, the moon, whose pale, yellow smile was reflected in the great liquid mirror. At this hour, everything exuded calm and serenity. Here and there, smoke rose from the thatched roofs : soon it would be light.

The protective moon had shone down on the young Sennait's hut, surrounding her with its benevolence, and the night itself had grown cottony, as if to muffle the painful moans of the young woman torn apart by the birth. Finally, in the early hours of the morning, the child was born, filling the silence with its vigorous cries. While the exhausted young mother rested on her bed, trying to regain her strength, the hungry baby suckled her enthusiastically, its big black eyes open to life. As for her mother, she stroked her little head of hair, smiling wearily and even a little sadly.

Meanwhile, on the other side of the village, a woman was busy. It was market day, and there was a long way to go. There was no time to lose : it would soon be hot. She went out into the early

dawn, accompanied by the crowing of the cocke-
rel and the barking of dogs. On the way, she paid
no attention to the beauty of the landscape before
her, preferring to concentrate on her steps. The
path was steep and dangerous, with frequent falls.
To see her like this, you'd have thought she was
an old woman, so hesitant was her gait. Her poor
canvas trainers, without laces, were far too big for
her feet, and didn't protect her from the sharp or
rolling stones. Wrapped up in a *shama*, she made
her way along, a ghostly figure in the early morning light.

When she reached the top of the hill, she paused
to catch her breath. A pain in her chest made her
wince. More and more frequent, these pains worried her, and although she was still young, the
Ethiopian felt it was time to "hand over the reins."
In fact, her own hands were beginning to tremble.
Yes, the time had come to talk to Mebrat, her
daughter-in-law. She allowed herself a few more
moments of respite before beginning the descent.

The huge market stretched out below. With her
eyes closed, Tsehaye let herself be carried for a
moment by the rumble that was coming up to her.
The place was buzzing with life : people were talking loudly, calling out to each other. Above all, this
market was a place for people to meet and exchange
ideas. The haggling of the customers was met by
the protests of the sellers. The laughter of children chasing each other barefoot in the dust, drunk
with freedom, was heard in the form of bells ; it

was echoed by the beaded laughter of the women, happy to be together and chatting in the shade of the tall trees, weaving wicker. The little ones, hanging from their mother's breast, slept, sometimes crying, bothered by the heat, the dust and the flies. To the cries of the men were added those of the animals they came to sell or buy. The outraged cries of the camels, the plaintive croaking of the goats and their young, the braying of the donkeys, the soft, throbbing mooing of the zebus... This deafening cacophony frightened the chickens, who clucked in panic at all the commotion. And yet, everyone here had their place, a well-defined place. Nothing was left to chance : it was a mess, but an organised one.

On the shores of the lake were the fishermen's quarters and the dugout canoe sellers. Made from eucalyptus, the long, light boats were piled up on the ground. People came from far and wide to buy them ; fast, they were perfect for gliding across the water. This was also the place to buy fishing tackle or have damaged equipment repaired. Finally, the fishermen's market was the meeting place for the kids who came there to sell their bounty, mainly tilapia and bearded bass, which abounded in the large lake.

A little further on, there were the butchers : zebu, goat or sheep meat, the bloody stalls in shades of red and soft pink excited flies and dogs. Chickens and guinea fowl, already plucked, waited there for all to see. Later in the evening, the cackling of the hyenas could be heard, who would not hesitate to chase away the enterprising vultures to feast on the remains of this long day.

In the shade of the tall trees, the women were selling their wares. A veritable palette that a distracted painter would have forgotten, this space seemed devoted to colour : carmine *berbéré* and sun-kissed *mitmita*, accompanied pepper and cardamom, as well as green and red chillies, brown cinnamon, black cumin, cloves and ginger. It was all there. In addition to the spices, there were red coffee beans, fragrant onions, cabbage, fresh garlic, shallots, green, blond and brown lentils, split peas, bananas and, of course, *teff*, which would be used to make *injera*. This was also the place to buy *khat* leaves, which would be chewed throughout the day. The heady scents mingled with the smells of fish and the bland, sickening smell of meat heated in the sun.

Further on, in a jumble, were baskets made of wicker, straw or zebu leather, headrests carved from wood, braziers for roasting coffee, earthen trays, wineskins, cooking pots, plastic jerry cans and other jerry cans, all very practical treasures for fetching water. It was also a paradise for coquettes looking for the dress or tunic, jewel or veil that would make them the most beautiful.

With her breath finally restored, Tsehaye set off again. She had an appointment with a little shepherd to collect the plants she would soon be using. Previously, she had done this herself. But that was no longer possible. She knew all their secrets, how to bring down fevers and soothe stomach aches. She knew how to get rid of worms, how to cure dysentery, how to get rid of lice and how to fight certain diseases. Sometimes, on rare occasions, people would ask her for advice. Tsehaye was the village cutter.

***

Squatting in front of a small brazier, young Mebrat was preparing coffee. That morning, as so often, the young woman was feeling sad and distraught. Last night, once again, she had been unable to respond to her husband Yared's advances. And, as always, she was dying of grief and resentment. Free and passionate, everything about her exuded sensuality : her gingerbread skin, her hips that she loved to sway, her high breasts, though weighed down by her new motherhood. Her full mouth was made for kissing ; her hands for caresses, whether received or given. In the privacy of their home, she loved to look at her husband, his muscular body, slim yet solid, his arms that knew how to embrace her. She loved his virility and yet... she couldn't welcome him without gritting her teeth, without tears welling up in her eyes. She felt an intense frustration. Mebrat sensed the bliss of abandonment, but never achieved it. Yes, she would have loved making love if millennia of tradition hadn't forbidden her pleasure.

She had just turned seven. That morning, her mother had taken her to stay with a woman in the village. There were three of them. Three girls to whom nothing had been explained and who were initially very impressed, even a little flattered, by the solemnity and ceremony of the occasion. It was time for them to become women, they were simply told, and that sounded a bit like a promise. To do this, they had to go through the "ritual." They had been washed, to be "purified," because this part of themselves would soon be taken away from them. Then they had been placed on a plank, rough against their children's backs. Mebrat remembered the anguish she felt at the time and how her mother begged her : "Don't cry. A woman must not cry. Be worthy of your mother." So, she was blindfolded and her hands were tied. She only had time to see a woman bend over her with a razor blade in her hand before the blindfold was put on. Then... She would still wake up at night, her heart pounding. Not to cry... Not to scream... To remain dignified. To deserve her mother's pride. To be a tough, strong woman. Even today, so many years later, that pain was still with her. She had just turned seven and they had come for her...

Oppressed, Mebrat went out onto the porch of her hut. As always, the sight of the lake warming up under the first rays of the sun soothed her...

It was to the lake that she liked to confide her joys and sorrows. Her nightmares too. Mebrat appreciated this time of day, a truce in the wild and merciless nature. As she often did, the pretty young woman lost herself in contemplating the landscape. The great lake was now decked out in the colours of the rising sun. The islands, lascivious, so close and yet inaccessible, seemed to abandon themselves to the caress of the water. Some of them were off-limits to women, which only added to their fascination. Like a wonderful but inaccessible, forbidden garden.

The young woman sat up and took a deep breath. She was breathing in her African land. She would have recognised its fragrance anywhere. It was the scent of wind and earth, of life and death too. Mebrat loved living there. The city didn't attract her, never had. She preferred her pretty mud house, her little garden with a banana tree, some vegetables and *teff*. She was happy to have married Yared. He was a good husband, gentle, respectful and attentive. As well as fetching water, albeit out of sight – water is a woman's business – he also carried wood and built fires. He didn't get drunk with the other men when he went to sell his *pirogues* at the market, nor did he return with his eyes reddened from chewing too much *khat*. Life with Yared went smoothly, between fishing, canoeing and picking coffee. Coffee... For as long as she could remember, the young woman had been picking coffee. First with her mother, and now with her little Genet who accompanied her, strapped to her back. "Coffee is Ethiopia's treasure, and it's what binds people together," her mother was fond of telling her. She was firmly convinced of this. A flock of flamingos interrupted her reverie and, in an instant, the surface of the water turned pink with pleasure.

Mebrat spotted Yared coming back with the cans. He was about to go fishing and would be on the water all morning. His life was intimately linked to the great Nile. People invoked it and made offerings to it. As she often said, "What would coffee be without water ? And what would water be without coffee ?" Mebrat couldn't help but feel a twinge of sadness : she didn't like the idea of him going fishing on his own. After all, the lake not only belonged to fish, birds and fishermen, it was also the kingdom of hippos and crocodiles, which were far more dangerous. Yes, water gives life, but it can also take it away. Shaking her head, the young woman stood up slowly, holding her stomach. "I look like a lounging hippopotamus," she sighed.

As she looked around for Yared, she recognised her mother-in-law, old Tsehaye, in the distance on her way to the market. The young woman couldn't help shivering and thought of her friend Sennait who had just given birth. Unconsciously, she put her hand on her belly, which was already very round. She thought of the child to come and clenched her fists. It would be a little boy ; it had to be a male. He would be called Alemayehu. That was the name of Mebrat's father, a strong and fair man who had sadly died very young.

In front of her, little Genet, aged two, was playing, sitting on the floor. Her mother looked at her pensively. What would her life be like ? What kind of woman would she become ? Life can be so hard for women ; you have to be strong. The latter, feeling watched, gave her mother her best smile before setting off to chase a hen that had come a little too close. Soon the clucking of the child and that of the chicken mingled.

Mebrat took advantage of this moment to prepare her hairdressing kit, the comb and the butter to shine her frizzy hair. The ceremony was about to begin. It was a very pretty sight, this young woman sitting on her porch, her stomach rounded, her head bent forward. Before coating her hair with butter to give it all its shine, she untangled it with large, sweeping strokes. Then she made two plaits and braided them into headbands. She knew they would enhance the oval of her face. When Yared had left for the lake, she would visit Sennait and bring her incense and coffee...

***

"Sennait ? It's me, Mebrat..."
She gently pushed open the door and had to wait for her eyes to adjust to the half-light before she could make out the figure lying on her bed. Her friend greeted her with a smile. The smile showed the young mother's pride, but also the tiredness of the past hours. It had been a difficult birth.

"Her name is Moulou..." The voice was a little sad and disillusioned.

"Sennait", she's adorable !" exclaimed Mebrat as she took the child in her arms.

"She's a beautiful little girl ; you should be proud of yourself. But you're exhausted  ! Wait, I'll take care of you. Would you like me to make you a cup of coffee ?"

"I'd love one".

"Then I'll help you wash up. Poor Sennait, you look so weak. I'll look after you. Your little Moulou is really beautiful, you know."

Mebrat needed to keep busy and talk. She was afraid to let the silence settle in, as if she had unconsciously known what her friend was about to ask her. Accordingly, she lit the small brazier, threw a little incense on the embers, and got on with the coffee. Soon the room was filled with the sweet smell of incense and roasted coffee. The young woman straightened up her friend on her bed. The latter couldn't suppress a grimace.

"Wait, I'll help you." She went to fetch some fresh water and a sponge for her forehead. Mebrat felt sad for the young body that had been torn apart by childbirth. She thought back to old Tsehaye.

"Please... I wish it were you."

Mebrat stiffened.

"I have to prepare the ceremony..."

"Be quiet  !"

"Please. Old Tsehaye will probably come by later today and I have to give her a name. You're the only one I know here. You're my friend. As you said yourself, we're almost sisters. You can't refuse me that... Please, Mebrat."

The young mother handed her daughter to her.

"I want it to be you. I want you to be her 'eyes mother'."

Mebrat shuddered. Another little girl to be mutilated, to suffer, to suffer so much. But why ? In the name of what ? She would never, never get used to this cruel custom…

Her whole body, her whole heart as a woman, but also as a mother, rebelled against this tradition from another time.

"Sennait, you know what I think of this custom…"

"Yes, I do. But what can we do about it ? There's nothing we can do. We have no choice. We can't do anything against tradition."

"Of course we have a choice ! All you have to do is say no !"

"I can't say no. What would people think of me ? And what would they say about her later ? No, you know Mebrat, I can't refuse. And what's more, she's lucky… She won't be like us… She's a baby ; we were seven…"

"Lucky ?" Mebrat's eyes were now flashing. "But how can you say that ? We're cut, mutilated… Lucky ? I can't urinate without clenching my teeth ! Lucky ? Don't you suffer when you're alone with your husband ? No, Sennait, we're not lucky ! And you think it will be less painful for your daughter because she's a baby ?"

"But you did it for Genet…" Mebrat's voice was just a whisper.

"Yes, I did. And I'm sick of it ! And I'm ashamed

of myself every day when I'm washing her and I can hear her whimpering or crying. Yes, I did… and I blame myself every day. Her sobs are like stab wounds in my mother's heart. You see, Sennait, I pray every day that this tradition will finally come to an end."

"But if the child you're carrying is a girl…"

"I also pray that it's a boy," she murmured to herself, putting her hand on her stomach.

"But if it's a girl," continued Sennait imperturbably, "you'll do what I'm doing. Because we can't do otherwise. It's our role as mothers. It's our role as women."

"When tradition is bad, then tradition has to be changed !" Mebrat now shouted, revolted by such submission.

"Shhh… I beg you, don't shout like that. People will hear you."

"That's what I'm talking about : we have to make ourselves heard !"

And yet, in spite of everything, Mebrat accepted her friend's pleas also out of sheer exhaustion. What could she do, alone, against an entire village, against centuries of tradition ? She could do nothing. Unfortunately, there was nothing she could do, and soon there would be another victim of excision…

Thus, she stayed with her friend for part of the morning, helped her wash and did some housework, assisted by little Genet. Finally, she prepared the meal and offered to fetch some water. The friends hardly spoke to each other. The silence was heavy, the unease perceptible. Only the laughter of the little girl, who had gone to play in the courtyard, brought a little lightness to the situation. Moulou had woken up and Genet, curious, had entered the room. Like all little girls, she asked to take her in her arms, but Mebrat refused. Moulou was too small. "But I'm grown up now," the child protested. Sennait found the strength to smile. She felt better and was reassured. Everything would be fine now ; she was sure of it. Once again, she thanked her friend.

***

The ceremony took place five days later. Mebrat hadn't slept a wink all night and had been tempted a thousand times to change her mind. However, as tradition dictated, she had prepared the *genfo* and *tella*, the food that would be shared to celebrate the ritual. Some of her neighbours had been invited. As for the men, they were waiting in the courtyard.

When the cutter crossed the threshold of the hut, the silence grew heavy and Mebrat's unease intensified. Little Moulou, until then so calm, began to cry. Sennait now cradled her nervously, head bowed, not daring to look at her friend. Her mother's heart was breaking, yet she didn't dare oppose this act, which she considered monstrous. Tsehaye solemnly unrolled a piece of cloth and took out a razor blade. Mebrat remarked to herself that it must already have been used. Pain stabbed her in the lower abdomen, like a painful reminder. What are you doing, Mebrat ? Are you going to take part in this ?

Tsehaye prepared the ointment to be applied to the wound. Supposed to relieve pain, it was also intended to prevent haemorrhaging or other possible complications. When everything was ready, she beckoned Mebrat to come closer. As "eyes mother," her job was to hide the little girl's eyes during the ceremony. Another woman would hold her legs. For a moment, she thought she was going to faint. Nauseous, her stomach aching, she staggered to her feet and had to hold on to the doorframe to contain the trembling that had taken hold of her. She hated this moment and cursed herself for taking part in it.

"Mebrat...you promised me..."

Yes, she had promised. So she took a deep breath, took the little Moulou in her arms and went over to where Tsehaye was pointing. The child had stopped crying and was looking at Mebrat. Her intense gaze seemed to question her. "What are you going to do to me ?" She was also saying to Mebrat : "I trust you, look, I'm not crying any more." She was so young, so pretty, so fragile ; so innocent too. Once again, Mebrat thought she was going to faint. She felt guilty, as guilty as if it were her own hand inflicting this suffering on the innocent little girl. She glanced desperately at Sennait. She alone had the power to stop all this while there was still time.

"Please, Mebrat…"

Disregarding her repulsion, without thinking any further, the "eyes mother" approached Tsehaye, like an automaton, and placed the child on a table. As instructed by the cutter, she stood over the child's head and bent down towards her. She couldn't bear to look at Tsehaye. While Tsehaye was getting ready, Mebrat whispered in little Moulou's ear. She asked her to forgive her. Sorry for not having been able to convince her mother. Forgiveness on behalf of all mothers. She asked forgiveness for her little Genet. And finally, she asked forgiveness for herself, for not having been able to refuse...

The cry was heartbreaking. It spread like a wave of pain to Mebrat, who frantically caressed the little girl's face, her own tears mingling with those of the child. "Mihirati, mihirati," she kept repeating...

"What's going on ?" Sennait had shouted.

Before anyone else, her instinct had told her that everything was not going to plan. Her daughter was now whimpering. It was like a lamb looking for its mother ; a lamb sacrificed on the altar of tradition. Her cries, piercing at first, were now becoming weaker and weaker.

"What's happening ?" Her mother repeated.

From where she stood, Mebrat gazed at the scene, petrified at the blood pouring from the wound. It was the life that was inexorably escaping from the little victim, despite Tsehaye's ointments.

"She's bleeding too much," whispered the cutter at last. It's not normal.

Sennait, now in a panic, shouted and begged old Tsehaye "Why isn't your ointment helping her ? Why is she still bleeding ? What have you done, Tsehaye ?"

"Sorry, sorry."

Little Moulou died during the night. The women of the village surrounded the inconsolable young mother. Mebrat remained cloistered at home, unable to face her friend's gaze, unable to stop herself from feeling guilty...

***

The weeks passed, with days of solitude chained to sleepless nights. Mebrat remained obsessed by the cry of little Moulou, by that of Sennait. She was losing sleep and appetite. Moulou's gaze, so intense and so black, pursued her and haunted her. She questioned her night and day. What have you done, Mebrat ? Why did you let her do it ? If she hadn't agreed to be the eyes mother... perhaps Sennait would have refused the ceremony ?

Yared ended up worrying about his wife and spoke to his mother, who promised to come and talk to her. She certainly couldn't stay like that, crying, locked up, without seeing anyone, walled up in silence. She was even neglecting their little Genet, who was doing everything she could to make people take an interest in her.

"We need to talk, Mebrat."

Busy pounding *teff*, the young woman hadn't heard her mother-in-law's approach.

"You've put on weight. She'll be born soon now."

"She ?"

"You're carrying your child on your hips, it's going to be a girl."

Tsehaye put her hand close to her daughter-in-law's belly and she jerked back. She shuddered at the prediction. But she continued to grind the grain, avoiding looking at the cutter, refusing to see her hands. Tsehaye sat down beside her. It was the first time they had seen each other since Moulou's death.

"Your friend's little girl..."

"Her name was Moulou..."

"She shouldn't have died. You see, I'm not that old, but my hand is starting to shake. And I can't see as well as I used to. So I'm going to have to stop soon. The village is going to need someone to take over from me and I thought of you. You're the wife of my last son and I didn't have a daughter. You have to replace me. It's your role, it's tradition."

Mebrat gasped in surprise. With her heart in her mouth, she straightened up and gazed proudly into her mother-in-law's eyes.

"Never Tsehaye. Do you hear me ? Never Tsehaye. Don't count on me. You'll have to look elsewhere. I refuse to kill little girls."

Her tone was calm, clear and unmistakable.

Supporting her stomach, she stood up and went into her hut. She couldn't bear the sight of the old woman trembling. She continued to speak, arguing that she herself had not chosen this responsibility. Her own mother had instigated it. She couldn't refuse. That was the way it was, handed down from generation to generation. And when there was no daughter to take over, it was up to the daughter-in-law. Therefore, it wasn't a question of being for or against it, there was no choice. That was all.

But Mebrat decided to choose. Not to give in to fear. She would be the first woman to oppose the custom…

From then on, the relationship between the two women deteriorated. Tsehaye was vexed by her daughter-in-law's refusal, and Mebrat avoided her mother-in-law. After the little girl's death, she remembered a story that her father had told her. As a child, he had seen a troop of hyenas surround a giraffe giving birth. The poor animal was desperately trying to keep the scavengers at bay, while at the same time trying to give birth. But the smell of blood had aroused the beasts. The giraffe didn't stand a chance. He hadn't even been born yet and he was already the victim of hungry hyenas. Such was the savannah, "harsh and merciless," concluded her father as he stood up. Deep down, only Mebrat called her stepmother "the hyena." The way she hovered around pregnant women, waiting and watching for babies to arrive, stalking little girls, horrified her.

***

"You had nothing to do with it..."

"Of course I did, I should have convinced you. I should have refused... I beg your pardon." Mebrat couldn't meet her friend's gaze. She was stubbornly scanning the distance, beyond the islands. It was Sennait who had come all the way here. Yared had come to her in great secrecy and told her of his concerns. He no longer recognised his wife and was worried. That morning, Sennait decided to take the initiative. She knew what was eating away at her friend. And that only she could free her, relieve her.

"It was up to me to refuse. She was my daughter, not yours. I made that choice. She's dead now. It's just there's nothing we can do about that. It was written. There was nothing we could do to stop it."

This time, Mebrat stared at Sennait. A look of pain, mingled with grief and anger. Sennait noticed above all the mother-to-be's dark circles and her cheeks, which had deepened.

"I'm going to do your hair, it'll relax you, and... you need it. What do you say ?"

Mebrat seemed elsewhere... "Do you really believe that things are written and that they are immutable ?"

"Of course I believe it. Moulou certainly had to die. And there's nothing anyone can do about it."

Sennait took Mebrat in his arms to console her. "You don't have to apologise to us, Mebrat. It's not your fault and it's not Tsehaye's fault either. It's not her fault. She didn't want my daughter to die."

Mebrat shuddered. The two friends hugged tightly and Sennait, perhaps a little too cheerfully, asked her to pour her a cup of coffee before helping her to get dressed…

# The Seventh Day

"Congratulations, Mebrat, she's a lovely little girl. What are you going to name her ?"

Mebrat stifled a sob. When she came to her senses, the little girl had been attached to her breast. With her serious little eyes, she seemed to be asking her : I am your daughter. What kind of mother will you be ?

For the next two days, she refused visits from her neighbours. Forty-eight hours looking at the little girl, caressing her, crying too. It was on the third day, when she was washing the baby, that Mebrat made her decision. It had become obvious. She smiled at the perfect little naked body.

"No one will touch you, my pretty princess, my flower. I promise you that. Even if I have to run away with you, even if we have to leave everything behind. No one will harm you. Tsehaye's blade will not harm you. You will be a proud and whole woman. No, you won't be cut. I didn't have that courage for your sister, I'll have it for you. I'm not afraid anymore."

The next day, Tsehaye crossed the threshold of

the hut to prepare for the ceremony. Mebrat seemed strangely calm as she welcomed her, even though deep down inside her heart was beating wildly. No, little Shoayé would not be circumcised. There was no question of her being mutilated. She had made up her mind. Neither Tsehaye, nor Yared, nor anyone else would change her mind.

The cutter stared at her. Tradition was tradition. What would become of the custom if the mothers refused to abide by it ? And what would become of her, Tsehaye, if the custom was no longer respected ? What would become of her if her own daughter-in-law refused her for her child ? And then, what would be said about the little girl ? They'd point the finger at her and push her away. She would be a disgrace to the village and would certainly never find a husband...

Everyone knew that the act made women more timid, and kept them faithful. A prostitute. That's how she would be treated. And that's what she would probably become. No man would take her. Mebrat couldn't deny that. What decent mother would choose such a future for her daughter ? But Mebrat remained unmoved. What kind of mother would she be if she accepted to hand his little girl over to the razor blade ? Was poor Moulou's death not enough ? How many more girls would have to be sacrificed before people realised that this tradition was dangerous and barbaric ? She was determined, ready to stand up to the whole village. If she had to run, she would run. She would take a *pirogue* and hide on an island with the child. She would flee to Addis Ababa, to her brother. No, there was no need for Tsehaye to bring her equipment, Shoayé would not be cut.

When she realised Mebrat's determination to oppose her, the old woman stood up straight, threw her *shama* over her shoulders and walked out with her chin held high, furious. She immediately went to the banks of the lake where her son Yared was repairing his *pirogue*.

"My son, I've just come from your house. You need to talk to your wife".

Yared stopped his work. He knew this day would come.

"Yared, you have to reason with her. She won't let me operate on the girl. You've got to talk to her. You're the man. You have to decide, because your wife can't."

The youngest of five boys, Yared had always stood out. Freer and more modern too, he didn't look like his brothers. His mother understood this very quickly. Desperately, she had tried to channel this energy, but can you really divert the course of a river, she used to say when talking about him. Yared had become a strong-willed and ambitious young man. He had refused to join his brothers who had taken over the zebu herd from their father.

Instead of mooing, he preferred the song of the lake ; instead of the movements of the herd, the ballet of the flamingos. In the mornings, from dawn onwards, he devoted himself to fishing. He liked to go out when the village was still asleep. In the afternoon, when it was too hot to sail, he would build dugout canoes in the shade of the tall trees. Yared was a talented craftsman. His fine, light boats soon became famous in the region, and people came from far and wide to buy them. When his father died, while his four brothers shared his father's flock, he was already, at just over twenty, at the head of a flourishing business. A good match, he was much sought after.

It was Tsehaye who chose the young Mebrat for his son. She came from far away, a hundred kilometres to the north. The only heiress in the family, fatherless, the young girl came with a handsome dowry : half a dozen heads of cattle, some jewellery, a little land and a few acres of coffee trees. Mebrat's brothers had both died, so she was the only one left...

The young bride's arrival in the village was much talked about. The new couple stood out for their modernity. Although Yared and Mebrat had not chosen each other, they had at least "met." Tsehaye had taken a dim view of this. Mebrat was taking up too much space, and certainly not the space she had reserved for her. She wasn't exactly a submissive woman ; she didn't hesitate to give her opinion and she immediately settled into her new home. When she picked up the coffee, she laughed loudly with her friend Sennait and enjoyed singing the songs of their childhood. When little

Genet reached her second year, Mebrat told her husband she wanted to send her to school. She wouldn't need her to pick coffee and preferred her daughter to learn to read and write. Tsehaye rebelled against this new whim. Girls didn't need to go to school. Would Genet need to know how to read in order to collect coffee, help her mother with the housework and finally become a wife and mother ? Certainly not. Tsehaye saw school, and girls' education in general, as a real danger. Women didn't have to think, the men were there to make the decisions ; educating little girls meant giving power to the women they would become. Perhaps the power to say no. As always in these cases, Yared ended up stalling, Genet was still young, we'd see when the time came.

The evening of her altercation with her mother-in-law, Mebrat had spoken to her husband. She told him that she refused to have their little Shoayé mutilated. She appealed to his common sense, to the father he was, and finally to the lover. Wouldn't he have preferred to have a woman next to him, in his bed, who didn't suffer during their embrace, who could have responded to his advances and his desires ? Of course she could understand her husband's reticence, his fear and the weight of the village gaze, that of Tsehaye. Oh, she was no fool, she knew what people thought of her. Mebrat, the rebel... Yes, perhaps they were right after all. But nothing would change her mind. Little Shoayé would not be circumcised, and Mebrat would have to leave the village to do it. But Yared had reassured her. He would support her. Besides, he himself had never really understood the point of this tradition. Many men of his generation felt the same way. Attitudes were beginning to change. It was enough to realise that you could take your destiny into your own hands by refusing what seemed to be an inevitability. Mebrat could rest assured that he would be there, at her side, to face the rest of the village and, above all, Tsehaye, his own mother ! And who knows, maybe it would be the start of a big change ?

On the seventh day, Tsehaye returned to her son's house. Mebrat intervened, forbidding her mother-in-law to enter the house.

Hadn't she understood anything ? Nobody would touch their daughter. A few of the neighbours had gathered, curious and excited by what seemed to be an inevitable row. But the young mother didn't back down and soon had the whole crowd on her side. Yes, everyone was concerned !

"Wasn't the death of little Moulou enough for you ? It's high time we gave up this tradition that's killing our daughters !"

"When a tradition exists, it must be a good one ! Retorted an old woman, pointing her finger at her."

"We wouldn't have made our daughters suffer for nothing," added another. "It's the price you have to pay to become a good wife, upright and faithful, a respected woman."

The tone rose. Who was she to question this ?

Besides, she wasn't even from the village. Tsehaye supported what the elders were saying by shaking her head... Yes, who was she who refused to respect custom and who did she think she was ? Did she have the right to forbid her daughter from being part of the clan, the family of women who have gone through the ritual ? Wouldn't Shoayé be angry with her one day ? But Mebrat did not give in and the furious cutter had to turn back.

***

At first, the whole family was ostracised. Mebrat's stubbornness or Yared's attitude were not understood, and that hadn't stopped anything. It was all anyone talked about, the little girl who hadn't been circumcised. People looked at Mebrat when she went to the market, her little girl asleep on her back. We whispered, half disapprovingly, half admiringly : you had to admit that she had had courage. People laughed at Yared, never hesitating to question his virility, as he let his wife lay down the law. The women especially were talking. Soon, the village split into two clans, those who disapproved and the others, albeit fewer in number, who supported the young woman. Mebrat, for her part, did not give up. She never stopped explaining and arguing. You had to listen to her passion as the women gathered with their laundry on the banks of the lake. Her rage made her even more beautiful, and she proudly displayed little Shoayé for all to see. True to his promise, Yared accompanied her in what was now becoming a real battle. He didn't hesitate to talk about it with the other men in the village, especially the younger ones, standing up to them when necessary. When, sometime later, Tsehaye's blade was once again called upon, Mebrat tried until the last moment to convince the mother. But it was all in vain. Yared was even told that it was time he advised his wife to stop meddling in other people's affairs. So other girls were born, and the seventh-day ritual continued, even if the village changed cutters, Tsehaye's hand trembling more and more.

# Say No Even When It Is Not Convenient

One day, while working on his canoes, Yared was joined by Wendante, a very young man whom he considered to be a bit like his little brother. A little lost little brother, whom he had to guide and protect. A little simple-minded, he was often the target of mockery from more seasoned men. A few months earlier, Yared had offered to teach him his trade. The boy was quick to accept. He was a rather isolated young man. Very shy, he often sought the company of Yared, whose freedom, commitment and, above all, courage he admired. That day, Wendante seemed disturbed. He couldn't concentrate and couldn't weave the papyrus stems together to form a *tankwas*, a dugout canoe.

"I've already told you... you lay the papyrus stems flat along the central wooden stem... If there's no stake, how are you going to guide your construction ! Think about it..."

But there was nothing to be done... his clumsy hands were trembling. The young man looked as if he was going to cry.

"What's the matter with you ? I can see that you're not well. Are you in trouble ? The young people in the village ? I'll go and see them if you like. Don't let them get you down. Believe in your name, 'The Strong Man'... You have to believe in yourself Wendante."

"No, it's not that. It's my wife..."

She was pregnant and nearing term. This plunged him into an abyss of uncertainty. They were both so young, so inexperienced... Wendante seemed totally taken aback.

"How am I going to feed the child ? We've got nothing. Just a bit of land."

"It's good fertile soil. You're going to learn how to cultivate it... and also how to make dugout canoes. I can employ you if you like, I've got lots of orders. There won't be too many of us. You see, there's nothing to worry about. And Mebrat can help your wife. She's a good mother, she'll teach her the ropes. So don't worry."

"That's just it..." The young man was becoming increasingly uncomfortable. "My wife's mother doesn't want me to work for you. She says you might be a bad influence on us, because of your daughter…"

"And what do you think ? Your wife is going to give birth very soon. Have you discussed it ? What will you do if it's a girl ?"

"We have no choice..."

"No choice ? Why not ? To be like the others ? So as not to upset your mother-in-law ? And what will you say if your daughter dies under the blade ? That you had no other choice ? Or that it's women's business ? You see, that's where I disagree. It's also about men. And we have a choice."

Yared was now looking at him sternly. Perhaps the time had come to prove that he too could be wise and courageous. Wendante "the strong man". He had to talk to Abeba, his wife ; they had to make their decision together. Yared knew that the mother-to-be had already spoken to Mebrat ; like her husband, she was reluctant to brave her community. Threats, pressure... The young woman's mother harassed the young couple, promising a thousand evils and even disinheriting them if they chose to join what were now known as "the rebels" : Mebrat and Yared. "No whores in the family," she hissed through her teeth, in a stream of contemptuous saliva. The young woman couldn't sleep at night and was dreading the birth of her child, praying, like so many other mothers, that it would be a boy.

Yared gave his apprentice a friendly slap on the back. It wasn't for his mother-in-law to decide. She belonged to the older generation. It was up to the new generation to choose what was best for them. Of course, you had to respect your elders, but you also had to accept progress.

"The decision is yours, Wandante. No-one else's. And you won't be alone. Mebrat and I are here. Shoayé too. You see, I don't think my daughter will be a bad woman, unfaithful or fickle. We're bringing her up to be an upstanding woman, just as we're bringing up her sister. There's no difference between the two. Take my word for it. There's no doubt about it. Your daughter will not be a whore if you refuse the ritual."

"And the others ?"

"More and more parents are making the same choice as us, and as I was saying, we men have our part to play. It's up to us to convince the parents of unborn girls that we will accept them as wives for our sons. Tell me, it's just us, no one can hear us..."

Yared's tone became more intimate. "When you're alone with your wife, isn't it difficult for her to join you ? Wouldn't you like to have a wife who doesn't suffer when she's alone with you in your arms ? Doesn't this suffering, even if our wives hide it from us, bother you ?"

"Why are you talking to me about this," replied the young man, suddenly very embarrassed. I don't see the connection...

"Can it be that you're so naive ?" interrupted Yared. "You see, I'm happy when I think that Shoayé won't suffer when she becomes a woman, when she gives herself to a man and it will be less painful and less dangerous for her to give birth. And I'll be proud to have been part of that. Think about it."

Yared was able to convince the father-to-be, who decided to act like a strong and courageous man. He decided to stop trembling and to stand up, with his wife, to the anger of his family. And so a second little girl was spared. As he had promised the young father, Yared gave him a job and Mebrat and Abeba became very close. The young couple moved in with their new friends.

Every morning, Yared left with Wandante. He taught him everything he needed to know to make beautiful canoes, and even introduced him to fishing. From then on, he would never venture out onto the lake alone, much to Mebrat's delight. The women, for their part, looked after the girls and the coffee together. Mebrat felt responsible for her new friend. The Wandante family had carried out their threat : the two young parents were no longer welcome in their home. They had been "contaminated," it was said, and had themselves become rebels. Let them keep to themselves.

Nine months later, Mebrat gave birth to her first son. Secretly, she thanked her lucky stars. The long-awaited little Alemayehu had finally arrived, a handsome, lively, plump little boy. He looked very much like Mebrat's father, and that pleased her. Twins were still to be born, one of whom would not survive. So the family now consisted of Genet, Shoaye, Alemayehu and Mesfin. It was a pretty family, happy and united. But Genet was suffering. She felt apart, different, isolated and sacrificed too. She envied her friends who got on with their sisters. She couldn't manage it. The more time passed, the wider the gap between Genet and her sister grew…

Shoayé was growing up, the object of everyone's attention, curiosity and slander. Every difference, every character trait, every flaw that could be attributed to her "peculiarity" was hunted down. Very quickly.

The little girl sensed this animosity. More than anything, she suffered from her elder sister's attitude. Genet, who had overheard a discussion between her parents, had asked her mother about her sister's "difference." Mebrat explained in very evasive terms. They would talk about it again when she and Shoayé were older and old enough to understand. She would have liked to have had a normal childhood, and for her family not to be the focus of gossip. Distant and haughty, she was the first to nickname Shoayé "kinteram," a rather vulgar term she had heard in the village for girls who had not been circumcised. She whispered it from the tip of her lips, in a mocking voice full of contempt. Shoayé began by resenting her mother for all the anger around her, which she didn't understand.

Years went by before Mebrat decided to explain everything to her. That afternoon, once again, Shoayé had returned from the lake in tears. A group of girls, led, of course, by Genet, had pushed her into the water. "Kinteram, kinteram," they sang at the top of their voices, preventing her from getting up, despite her cries and screams. The little girl had to wait for the girls to run away before making her way back to shore. She came home an hour later, soaking wet and barefoot. Genet, who had already returned, was helping her mother roast the coffee. She smirked when she saw her sister arrive.

"Mum, what does 'kinteram' mean ?"

"You're soaking wet ! And where's your shoe ? Where did you hear that word ?"

Mebrat pulled her close. Shoayé refused to answer. What she wanted was to understand. So Mebrat spoke.

She explained the ritual of the seventh day, the suffering that never really left those who had been circumcised. She told her about her incessant nightmares, the memory of the board under her kidneys, her tears of pain and Genet's tears. Then there was Moulou's death, which had shattered Sennait and continued to haunt her, who had agreed to be her "eyes mother." Finally, there was the anger that had overwhelmed her and never left her. Shoayé had to understand that she had nothing to be ashamed of, quite the opposite. She was the first, of course, but she was no longer the only one. Since then, there had been the little girl from Wandante and Abeba, and another, in a neighbouring village. Mebrat caressed her daughter's face.

"Flowers aren't meant to be cut," she added with a gentle smile.

It was at this very moment that little Shoayé decided to join her mother in her fight. And every time she heard herself called by her nickname, every time she received an intrusive look, she stood up straight, and with all the pride she felt capable of and that carried her, she repeated the phrase that had now become her own : "Flowers are not meant to be cut."

# Standing Firm Against All Odds

A handful of children were chatting happily on the path by the big lake. They were hurrying so as not to be late. They weren't discouraged by the five kilometres they had to cover. They were proud to be going to school, aware of how lucky they were. Not all the children in the village went to school. The others stayed in the fields, looked after the cattle or fished on the lake. The little girls helped their mothers with the housework, looked after the younger children and the farmyard, picked coffee or sorted it, and so learned to be good wives and mothers in the future.

The school was a building made of earth and metal sheets. It was home to a few young people of all ages. They were taught the basics, how to count and read, and how to write for the bravest. The old master, Ato Getatchew, was strict and would use a cane if necessary to calm down the unruliest. To the delight of some, he was soon replaced by a young, more modern teacher. The children soon called her Miss Lulit. She was a sweet and cheerful young woman. She did not hesitate to make her pupils sing, to teach them a few English basics and, finally, to meet with their parents when she felt it was necessary.

Miss Lulit believed in her job, and it showed. For Shoayé, their meeting was decisive. In her childish eyes, the teacher personified education and, above all, freedom. Single and childless, she didn't fetch water or carry firewood. There was no one to tell her what to do, or not to do...

Shoayé aspired to become a doctor. To make herself useful, to look after people, that was her dream. She was aware that to realise her dream, she would have to go far away. First to Addis Ababa, to continue her studies, and then perhaps even further away. But she was ready. Of course, she loved her lake, but she already knew that her life would be elsewhere.

As for Genet, she would be a coffee picker, like her mother. She wanted a quiet life by the lake. Unlike her sister, she didn't feel the need to leave. The girl was thirteen. Soon she would stop going to school and get married. She had explained this to their mother, who had nevertheless asked her to take her time, she was still so young. But the teenager insisted. She wanted to do what the other girls in the village were doing, finding a husband. Didn't Mebrat get married at fourteen ? The argument was unstoppable. With her friends from class, she looked at the boys, wondering which one might become her husband.

There was the handsome Mulugeta, who she liked

a lot. He was a tall young man in his twenties. He tended his father's flock nonchalantly. The young man knew he was handsome. When they met in the village, she would look away, falsely modest, and go off with her friends, laughing a little too hard ; he would ignore her, vaguely haughty. Genet wanted to get married, and fast. "I'm not like my sister, I don't want people pointing fingers at me."

She continued to suffer from the community's view of her family. Being Shoayé's sister was not easy. At an age when you don't want to stand out, she resented her mother for not having her sister circumcised. What would they say about her, what would they say about them ? A neighbouring family had even forbidden the two sisters to play with their children ! That day, she felt like shouting that it wasn't her fault. She had been circumcised ; she was just like the other girls ! She had ended up holding her sister responsible for all this, and she was ashamed of it. "When I have a little girl, I'll have her cut," she kept telling anyone who would listen.

***

One day while she was at school, a group of girls once again took Shoayé to task. A dozen of them surrounded her, pushing her around and laughing. Some spat.

The teacher came to Shoayé's aid. What had happened ? Shoayé told her about the hair pulling, the torn notebooks and the mocking laughter. The morning journey was particularly terrible and her own sister was one of the ringleaders. The little girl chose to trust the teacher. She knew her well and had a vague feeling that she, and the school in general, could be her allies. At the age of eleven, she had already understood that educating girls was essential : they would be the mothers and perhaps also the cutters of tomorrow.

A few days later, the schoolmistress called the girls together. Why were they harassing their classmate ? What did they know about female anatomy ? For the first time, the schoolgirls heard about the part of themselves they had been deprived of.

They finally understood and agreed to talk. They spoke of their pride in being circumcised, even though they suffered from it regularly. You had to accept it to be an honest woman. Were you a woman when you hadn't undergone the ritual, a woman worthy of finding a husband ? On the contrary, did they not become like the women who were paid off and hung around the towns, despised by everyone ? That's what they said back home. Were there countries where girls were not circumcised ? With a great deal of gentleness and patience, but also firmness, the teacher explained that there were countries where girls did not undergo this ritual. In fact, even in Ethiopia, not all girls were excised. It depended on the region, the beliefs and the family.

For the first time, Shoayé felt real pride. She caught herself thinking that it was the other girls who were "special," and that reassured her. After all, it was only a question of point of view. Yes, the lesson given by the teacher reassured her. It was possible to be "whole" and still succeed in life. She felt stronger. The other girls asked her more and more questions. Shoayé was a good pupil : were whole girls more intelligent ? The teacher reassured them with a smile. No, that had nothing to do with it. She concluded, insisting that their destiny was their own, and that of their future daughters. May they never forget it.

Soon debates were taking place within the school, a privileged space for exchanging ideas and listening. Mebrat, to whom Shoayé had reported what had been said in class, quickly made friends with Mademoiselle Lulit. Together, the two women organised "courses for women." In fact, it was more a question of time devoted to discussion. Not many women attended at first, and those who did were usually hidden away in their large *shama*.

Yared, for his part, continued to debate with the men. This was beginning to bear fruit. Already, when Abeba had refused to subject his daughter to the seventh-day ritual, his furious mother-in-law had not hesitated to complain to Aklilou, the village chief. Aklilou knew Yared well and had been a friend of his father. He liked the young man and valued his opinion. As a wise man, Aklilou was aware of what was happening in his village. It seemed the time had come for him to intervene, to appease the spirits. He asked Yared to join him one afternoon under the big tree by the lake. The generous tree offered its shade to anyone who wanted to take shelter there, and it was there that people liked to meet and chat.

The two men settled down comfortably, each leaning on his headrest. Aklilou, wrapped in his large white *shama*, gazed at the islands of the lake in the distance. An enlightened man, he loved solitude and often came here when he had something to think about, away from the noise of the village. He liked to say that he should ask the great lake for its advice. The two men, united in the same respect, soaked up the silence, disturbed only by the cries of the birds.

"Do you think, Yared, that it's a good idea to abandon a tradition ?"

"When a tradition no longer corresponds to society, then I think you have to know how to abandon it. The world is changing. We can imagine another ritual that wouldn't hurt our daughters... Because that's what you want to talk to me about, isn't it ?"

A discussion ensued. Each listened to the other and argued. Traditions were the glue that held societies together, and if they were no longer respected, wouldn't that be dangerous for their age-old identity ?

"What will people think of me if I leave you and Mebrat to it ?

"That you're a wise and modern chief," retorted Yared. And it's as such that you have to set an example. Aklilou's wife was carrying their eighth child. What would they decide if it was a girl ? Yes, men had to be concerned too. Excision was not just a women's issue. It was everyone's business. Other parents would join them, Yared was sure of it. He took up his wife's phrase : "Flowers are not made to be cut." Aklilou could play his part in this, as a visionary and enlightened leader, and why not, as a father. One of the arguments in favour of the custom was the fear of not finding a husband. It was up to them, the future spouses, to make it known that this was no longer the case.

The village chief, being a reasonable man, chose to favour community dialogue. And so, thanks to his wisdom, discussions could take place, and people could freely express their ideas.

***

A little girl was born to old Aklilou, and her parents decided to spare her. This decision caused a veritable earthquake in the village and surrounding area. As a wise man, Aklilou had decided to set an example. A few weeks later, it was Sennait's turn to refuse the ritual. She had finally found the courage and strength she had lacked for little Moulou. This courage had transfigured her : she was proud of it. She would save her daughter. Sennait was nothing like the shy, fragile young woman who always seemed to apologise. She would no longer be burdened with guilt over the death of her little Moulou. Two other women from the village soon followed suit. Mebrat was shocked to see all these changes : she was upset and proud. At last, something was happening ! Oh, she wasn't fooled, it would be a long time yet. But all the same !

***

The village continued to evolve. Young women, encouraged by Mebrat, Abeba and now Sennait, attended meetings at the school. Discussions became freer and freer. Yared and Wandante spoke to the young men, future husbands. Of course, Chief Aklilou's decision had left its mark on the clan.

Genet continued to be hostile. If generations of mothers had decided to have their daughters excised, it was because it was necessary. There couldn't have been that many of them who'd been wrong for so long... No matter how much it was explained to her that it wasn't a mistake, there was a more obscure, more intimate reason for her reaction. Genet couldn't bear the idea that Mebrat had refused to circumcise her youngest daughter out of love... What was she to think, she who had undergone the ritual ? Had her mother loved her less ? Had she deserved less to fight for her ? Genet was jealous, with a dull jealousy that suffocated her, poisoned her existence and her relationship with her youngest daughter.

So when it was her turn to give birth to her first daughter, the very next day she had the cutter called in to prepare the ceremony. When she heard the news, Mebrat ran to her daughter's house. How could this be ? Had she understood nothing of their fight, or learned nothing ? Genet, through clenched teeth, replied that it had never been her fight. Besides, her mother had had her circumcised...

At these words, Mebrat's heart sank. She took her daughter in her arms. She began by asking her daughter to forgive her. If Shoayé should not be ashamed of not being circumcised, the same was true for her, Genet. Both were women in their own right and she was proud of both her daughters. Mebrat had not dared to oppose Tsehaye when she was born. She was still so young, and so alone, too. She had wanted the best for Genet and had therefore decided to follow the custom, as her own mother had done for her. And then, she had seen her suffer, had heard the poor, seven-day-old, screaming in pain. She instantly regretted her decision. She had cried when hearing her moan. When, three years later, little Moulou died under the cutter's blade, Mebrat had made up her mind. She would never again impose the ritual and, from now on, she would refuse to be an "eyes mother." Unfortunately, the past could not be changed, but Genet could work for her daughter's future : she too could refuse.

In the end, it was after a long, tearful discussion, tinged with anger and resentment, that Genet gave up the idea of having her little girl excised...

# France, in the 2010s

# Mebrat's House

Lost in the contemplation of her wardrobe, Dr Haile looked pensive. In the end, she opted for black trousers and a simple white blouse with a slight slit. For jewellery, she wore a gold chain on which hung a small Coptic cross, and a fine gold embossed bracelet, a gift from her mother when she graduated. A little powder on her eyelids, a light line of lip liner : Shoaye was superb. She was the perfect embodiment of that haughty, feline African beauty. As the guest of honour at the "Medicine in the Third World" seminar...

She had never liked social occasions, so she was initially tempted to refuse this "honour," but she was delighted, seeing in this event, which was certainly very distressing for her, an opportunity to make Mebrat's House known to as many people as possible. The conference would have an international following... It would have been stupid to miss out on such an opportunity.

In Deauville, on the Normandy coast, in front of the Hôtel des Planches, there was a flurry of activity. There was a veritable ballet of cars. Eager

drivers opened the doors to doctors from all over
the world. For a few days, they would be exchanging ideas, analysing, and even trying to seduce
because treatment is expensive. It was going to be
necessary to convince people and to obtain the
financial help of generous benefactors, patrons
and philanthropic sponsors, with this ever-haun-
ting question : how much does the life of a child
cost ?

Yes, the programme was ambitious, and admitte-
dly, even if it was painful, it had to be acknowledged
the planet was not doing so well. Doctors were
going to talk about vaccination campaigns, mos-
quito nets, treatments, HIV and epidemics. They'd
also be talking about local training, girls' education, hygiene and contraception. The journalists
soon arrived. The specialist meetings were not
scheduled until the following day, but the opening,
including Dr Haile's speech, would take place that
evening, just before dinner. In the meantime, everyone settled down in the main hall. A short report
on the region was shown, and the beauty of the
D-Day beaches was admired. The room was still
bathed in half-light when she arrived, accompanied to the podium by the President of the seminar. A microphone and an armchair were waiting
for her.

When all the lights came back on, the young
woman stood petrified for a moment. Everyone
was struck by her beauty, which was in no way dimi-
nished by her embarrassment – quite the opposite,

in fact. Shoaye Haile thought of Mebrat's House and all those who counted on her. She thought of her mother and sat up straight. The shambling gazelle gave way to the Abyssinian Queen.

The chairman approached and introduced her to the audience : Dr Haile, "female genital reconstruction surgeon." Shoaye began with a brief history of the practice of excision. It was important to understand in order to be able to act. Too often, people were too quick to make judgements. Did we know, for example, that the famous Ambroise Paré, often regarded as the father of surgery and surgeon to King Charles IX, advocated cutting off the clitoris, which was seen as a pathology at the time, and that in the 19th century, excision was still attracting the attention of European learned societies ? Excision was not confined to the African continent, even today. A medical presentation followed. The surgeon presented the four types of female genital mutilation that have been identified. She then detailed the countless repercussions of these practices, then spoke of the need to relieve the victims.

Dr Haile was on fire, and the doctor in her took a back seat to the woman. Some in the audience shuddered. It was time to present Mebrat's House, a reception centre opened in Addis Ababa by Shoayé and Mebrat a few months earlier. It was a small private clinic where she worked to give women back a part of their intimacy and relieve them of abominable pain. It was important to understand that these women had to rebuild themselves physically, but also psychologically. The memories of the ritual were also painful. Shoaye Haile's aim was for other clinics to open around the world where women continued to be mutilated in this way. Therefore, she needed everyone's support and goodwill.

Finally, Shoayé insisted on the importance of educating both girls and boys. In fact, when she wasn't treating them, she went out to meet younger people in secondary schools and at Medical School. She remained convinced that if things were to move forward, people had to be able to speak out. When she finished her speech, the audience rose to its feet, first in respectful silence, then bursting into applause. Shoayé had won her bet.

***

"Doctor, a journalist has asked to meet you."

Dr Haile looked up from her file and paused, clearly annoyed : she had no time... However, she changed her mind : journalists could be her allies. She was on her way.

Mebrat's House France was designed to open its doors to women in turmoil, women whose flesh and soul had been tested. Shoayé had dreamt it up, then patiently created it with determination. The entrance consisted of a large room divided into small lounges with a few *mossob*, Ethiopian tables made of woven straw, wooden stools, a few armchairs and sofas, too. There was also a bar, with a small fridge and microwave oven. On the beige walls were photos of the Ethiopian high plains and posters with slogans praising the land of the Reine of Sheba : "Ethiopia, thirteen months of sunshine." The windows were draped with light veils and *shama*. Everything was done to make each woman feel protected and sheltered, with the possibility of staying for a while to treat her wounds and think about her future life.

Here they could talk, confide in each other, and at last, put words to their suffering. Behind the reception area, there was a photo of the head office in Addis, with the team gathered on the porch. A map of the world was displayed on the wall, showing the many countries where excision is still practised.

Initially intended to welcome mutilated women who came here to rebuild their lives, Mebrat's House gradually became a refuge for women who had been abused or raped. A full-time team was available to welcome and support them : doctors, psychologists, two social workers, and, of course, the team worked hand in hand with a group of lawyers to guide these women through the process when they decided, increasingly frequently, to lodge a complaint. Shoayé had even managed to win over a clinic to her cause. She now had a surgical theatre where she could operate on her patients. Yes, she was really proud of this facility, and rightly so.

When the surgeon entered the room, the young

journalist was looking at the photos on the walls. One of them seemed to catch her eye.

"This is my mother. Mebrat. She's beautiful, isn't she ?"

"You look a lot like her. Mebrat, like Mebrat's House ?"

"We can't hide anything from you."

The young woman laughed at the stupidity of her question and held out her hand.

"My name is Reine Pardon. Like forgiveness. I could have been a nun with a name like that. But then, I preferred to be a journalist."

Reine Pardon had written about women in the Resistance, both famous and unknown, and was proud to have met Simone Veil, whom she admired above all others. A feminist activist, she wrote about the Minister's commitment and her fight to decriminalise abortion. Her pen had always been dedicated to the cause of women.

She immediately appealed to the surgeon. Blonde hair in disarray, jeans that were no longer the freshest, a cheeky look that no line of make-up highlighted, a frank smile ; she was a ball of energy that exuded benevolence. Shoayé, amused, showed her guest to an armchair.

"You wanted to meet me ?"

"Yes, excuse me. I wouldn't want to waste your time. You know, I was in Deauville. I heard your speech ; I was in the audience. You impressed me. You were so... how shall I put it... so... I can't find the words.

Shoayé was touched by this admiration.

"I'd like to write something about you. About you. For the women you fight for."

"Really ?"

The surgeon accepted the offer. Reine Pardon was expecting to have to argue. But she didn't.

# Understanding to Fight Better

The two women got into the habit of meeting regularly. They often met in Shoayé's office, sometimes in town, in a restaurant or on a café terrace.

The journalist spoke to women, young and old, who had come to Mebrat's house seeking comfort, women who were in pain, and often lost. She was moved by a Guinean student who had come with her nine-year-old sister. She had overheard her parents talking to her grandmother at the *Place de la Madeleine* : they were going to take advantage of the forthcoming holiday in the country to have the youngest child circumcised. The desperate student was ready to do whatever it took. But what could be done ? That day, Reine Pardon realised the scale of the task ahead.

Shoayé had met the little girl's mother several times. She had argued for hours. The child had been born in France, so she had nothing to do with this tradition. The mother, a modern, independent woman, would have none of it. As for the grandmother, although she had lived in France for over fifteen years, she had always associated her roots with tradition. In her eyes, refusing to accept the customs of her country would be tantamount to breaking away from them. A bit like an infidelity. Besides, a large part of her family lived back home and wouldn't have understood if the little girl hadn't followed the custom. The little girl had to remember where she came from. Guinea were her roots. She wouldn't die from it ; other girls had been there, others still would !

It was all very well for the surgeon to assure her that it *was* possible to die from it, that the practice was forbidden, that her attachment to her country of origin could be expressed in other ways : through learning the language, through fashionable clothes, poetry or music, in short through anything cultural... but there was nothing she could do.

On the morning of the departure, Shoayé went to ring the doorbell, but it was the father who turned her away, just as her mother had been turned away in the past. Heartbroken and full of rage, she had to let the child go. Totally demoralised, she called the journalist to whom she had promised to give news.

"What if we had dinner together ? I'll invite you to my place. Ethiopian meal. I don't feel like spending the evening alone." Reine Pardon, surprised, accepted without hesitation.

That evening, she arrived with a bouquet of flowers in her hand. The Ethiopian thanked her, a little confused. It was the first time a woman had given her roses. For the evening, she had put on a traditional dress. Long, white and embroidered with gold thread, it showed off her waist to its best advantage. Her frizzy hair, which she took great care of, shone in the light. An embroidered veil covered her shoulders. She was barefoot and Reine Pardon found it hard to recognise the shy, anxious young woman she had met a few weeks earlier in Deauville. She was definitely the Queen.

"I was just preparing dinner. Come in. Let's go into the kitchen. I'll show you the *injera*. Waiting on the kitchen table were the *teff* cakes that would soon be adorned with culinary preparations, each more delicious than the last.

"Breathe it in." The young woman lifted the lid of a pot.

"This is *dorowat*, chicken in sauce with hard-boiled eggs. It's a bit spicy, but it's delicious. There's ginger, berbere, chilli, but not too much, don't worry... Here you have *mesir wat*, a lentil-based recipe ; I've also prepared some meat wat for you. It's a bit like your beef stew. Of course, you'll have to try the *niter kibbe*, which is a kind of butter. It's sautéed with onions, garlic, ginger and spices. Then it's clarified. It's delicious. What do you say ? Would you like to try it ?"

Reine couldn't take her eyes off the food. The aromas had taken hold of her and carried her far away. A few minutes later, the two women sat down to eat.

"We don't have cutlery or plates here. You'll have to eat with your hands," explained the young

Ethiopian woman, smiling. The *injera* is the dish, but it's also the utensil.

She unrolled a wafer onto a circular tray, placed the various preparations on top, tore off a piece of wafer and helped herself to the dish. She took some lentils and offered it to her guest.

"It's tradition, the *gursha*. My way of wishing you bon appétit and honouring you."

The journalist was seduced and let herself be tempted. A few moments later, they were laughing together. *Injera* was undoubtedly a dish for sharing, for reaching out and touching hands, for exchanging laughter and for budding friendships.

After the meal, the two women sat down on small wooden stools and Shoaye concentrated on the coffee she was about to serve. The coffee ceremony – *buna* – was a serious matter in Ethiopia, and the surgeon wanted to honour the journalist. In accordance with tradition, she had laid out all the necessary ingredients in front of them : a small brazier, charcoal, the small pot in which the incense would soon be burning, the mortar, the pestle used to crush the green coffee beans, a small earthen bowl, two small cups without handles, the coffee pot and its stand. Not forgetting the salt, sugar and butter to go with it, as well as toasted barley beans and *dabo*, Ethiopian bread.

Reine Pardon watched attentively. Perhaps she was thinking about her latest model machine and the pods that sat on the bar in her American-style kitchen. She couldn't help feeling a little ashamed.

Her thoughts turned to her dead grandmother. She saw herself as a little girl, grinding coffee under her grandmother's benevolent gaze. Where had that little wooden grinder gone that she loved to handle ? She promised herself that she would go and look for it in her grandparents' house, which had been left a bit abandoned since they left. She knew where her grandmother kept it. With a bit of luck, it would still be there.

"I rinsed the beans several times beforehand. Now they're ready to be grilled," said Shoayé, laying them out on the brazier. She was busy as she spoke.

"Once they're toasted, we can crush them. Can you smell that ?"

She leaned gracefully over to the wooden tray, grabbed the coffee pot and poured the brew into the cups. Near them, in a pot set aside for the purpose, incense burned, giving off blue wisps. Reine Pardon felt transported, once again, thousands of kilometres away. She imagined herself in a small mud house on the Abyssinian high plateaux, similar to the photo hanging in the entrance hall of her hostess's flat.

Finally, the two women settled down comfortably and Shoaye accepted the cigarette offered to her by Reine Pardon.

"Would you like to tell me about it ? Would you tell me exactly what you do for a living ? And also, above all, why this practice is so dreadful."

The Ethiopian sank further into her sofa and,

as usual, propped a cushion against her stomach, perhaps as a way of protecting herself from what she was about to say. There was a heavy silence during which she plunged into deep thought. Her gaze followed the smoke escaping from her half-open lips. The journalist looked at her intensely, hanging on her lips. Shoayé began to tell her story, choosing her words carefully, weighing them with a thousand precautions ; as if not to offend Reine, and perhaps also not to offend her own memory. She took a long breath and then launched into the story of the ceremony during which her mother had been circumcised, at the age of seven, along with other little girls her age. The words were grave and painful, heavy with the mute screams of the female children. Reine Pardon shivered as Shoayé went on, stiff, with a stern look in her eyes and a clenched jaw. The Ethiopian now seemed to be speaking for herself. She was far from her flat, far from her guest, lost somewhere on the shores of a lake.

"But why all this ? I've never understood the reason for it. It seems so... barbaric..."

"It's never easy to understand the reason for a tradition. It's an age-old tradition, and contrary to what some people believe, it's not necessarily linked to religion. The proof is that the first recorded cases of excision date back to the Egypt of the pharaohs ! My own family is Christian, yet the women in my family have been excised ; as for my grandmother, she was one of the most renowned cutters in the region. Removing the clitoris means taking away a part of a young girl's body that is considered 'masculine,' and thus enabling her to become a woman. As for the suffering, even if it is excruciating, it enables the woman to become stronger. At least that's what mothers say. You say that "what doesn't kill makes you stronger.' It's the same thing for women who perform excisions or have them performed. A woman who can endure this pain will be respected in her community, will have suitors and will be a good wife and mother. Suffering is not denied, on the contrary. In the minds of women, it is unfortunately seen as a necessary step. It is an integral part of the rite, and if parents have their daughters excised, it is to avoid them being singled out and denigrated. Uncut girls were, and still are, sometimes associated with prostitution. It's for their own good, in a way ; for their reputation and for the honour of the family.

"Yes, but sometimes excision kills."

"Yes, sometimes."

"It's so... I'm sorry, but it just seems so... cruel... so... barbaric, I'll say it again..." The journalist was at a loss for words, so monstrous what was being explained seemed to her.

Shoayé continued :

"Be careful, these women don't deserve to be judged. You have to learn not to judge, even when you don't understand, especially when you don't understand. Remember what I explained at the conference. Excision is a profession, even if it is now illegal in the vast majority of countries where it is practised. Cutters have a real social status and it is not by spitting our contempt in their faces that the problem will be solved. On the contrary, it will be solved through community dialogue, with the chiefs, religious leaders, the elderly and, of course, women. The West must not simply condemn and claim that 'it's not right,' but simply denounce and describe the custom as barbaric, to use your term. Besides, we mustn't forget that the women who practise excision are also victims ; my grandmother suffered too. She cried too.

"So why go on ?"

"You have to know that you can stop…"

"Let me ask you a… delicate question. If I'm being indiscreet, don't answer. You…"

"You want to know if I've been circumcised. No. In fact, I should have been, but my mother refused. I'm the first girl in my village not to have been mutilated. Thanks to my mother. She even threatened to go and hide."

"She even threatened to go and hide on one of the islands in the lake…" she added with a smile, one of the islands where women were not allowed.

Shoaye told her about her mother's courage, the death of little Moulou and Mebrat's decision.

"Mebrat the rebel…You can imagine that this was considered an affront to the community. My grandmother, who was a cutter, demanded that I undergo the ritual, but my mother stood her ground. She refused the ceremony. Later, she sent me to school with my sister Genet. You know, in my language, Mebrat means 'the light.' Never has a first name been so well known."

"Does Genet live in France ?"

"No, she lives there, by the lake. She married a zebu farmer and picks coffee. We don't have the same background. Genet is my elder sister. She was circumcised and I think she's always resented my 'singularity.' That's also why I left for Addis Ababa, the capital. I wanted to go to school, get an education, learn other languages and choose my life. My uncle was a caretaker at Guebre Mariam, the Franco-Ethiopian secondary school. He and his wife agreed to take me in, and I was able to go to school there. That's how I was able to learn French. Anyway, I couldn't really stay in my village on the banks of the lake any more. I can't thank my parents enough for listening to me and understanding me.

She recounted her adolescence in Addis, living with her aunt and uncle. She had been happy with them. They had taken her in like their own daughter. They were simple, generous people. For the first time in her life, Shoayé had her own room. She helped her aunt with housework, learned to sew and looked after her six-month-old youngest child. And then, of all things, she was able to go to secondary school. She loved this period of her life. The high school was a truly cosmopolitan place, a cultural crossroads where some forty nationalities were represented. To be a teenager at the

Guebre Mariam High School was to have access to the world. There, at last, there were no more contemptuous nicknames, no more coy laughter. Shoayé was a schoolgirl like any other. She showed her guest a photo hanging on the wall. It showed a group of smiling teenagers sitting on the bleachers in front of a stadium : friends who were happy to be alive.

"It's a lovely photo. Are you still in touch ?"

"Unfortunately, not. It has to be said that we were of different nationalities. We came from all over the world. What a joy it was to share those moments, and what a richness too ! Today, of course, we're scattered all over the place. As for those bleachers… They were the sacred place of the high school ! We met there, we chatted there, we courted there too. The boys would parade in front of the girls, who would laugh and look away. There we had our first feelings, first flirtations, and sometimes first sorrows."

It was on these very bleachers that she had thought out her life, dreamt it and organised it. She would become a gynaecologist and devote her life to women. Much later, while studying in France, she heard about reconstructive surgery.

"Did other women join your mother in her fight ?"

"Yes, even if it took a long time. There were other women who also chose to preserve their little ones."

"But how can you 'reconstruct' - that's the term

I think you use - a woman who has been excised ? It's impossible, isn't it ?"

Not at all ! The surgeon regained the upper hand. It all depends on the type of excision the woman has undergone. Reconstruction can enable an organ to be recreated by freeing its base. Unfortunately, this is not always possible. The first young woman I reconstructed calls me her second mother. It's a rather strange relationship, in fact... I've become her godmother... but every advance can also have a negative impact, every coin has its flipside. Today, for some, the argument is that you can excise and respect tradition because it's possible to repair, especially as some doctors suggest excising under anaesthetic... As if the only problem was the pain of the procedure !

Reine drank in her words, overwhelmed and admiring. Her own life seemed dull. What use was she to others ?

"Do you want to help me ?" Shoayé seemed to have read her guest's mind. "I'm due in my village in three weeks. Come with me. I'll introduce you to Mebrat and Genet. Do a report on my mother. She's the light, she's the heroine.

The journalist agreed, excited at the prospect of this trip and the meetings to come, moved by this mark of confidence.

"In the meantime, this evening, I need something light... *ulet bira* ! That means two beers..." she said, rising to her feet. "You're going to try Ethiopian beer. And then we're going to dance. I'm going to teach you. That way, you'll be initiated and ready when we get there."

She stood up and disappeared for a few moments, returning with a dress in her arms.

"Go and put this on. You need it to dance well. And it will change you ! I've never seen you in anything but jeans ! Come on, I'll wait for you ! In the meantime, I'll go and get us some beers."

Reine, uncomfortable, complied. She reluctantly abandoned her old, torn jeans for a beautiful traditional dress, embroidered in the colours of Ethiopia. She looked at herself in the mirror and immediately felt ridiculous. But she straightened up and tried to smile. She picked up the *shama* and tried to place it on her shoulders, as she had seen the Ethiopian woman do.

"Wait, I'll help you." Shoayé was behind her, Reine hadn't heard her coming.

"I'm ridiculous..."

"Don't think that, on the contrary, I think you're splendid and very... sexy. Wait, I'll help you." She laid out the stole. The touch of the cotton veil on her bare shoulders and Shoayé's light breath on the nape of her neck increased the journalist's confusion, and she felt herself blushing.

"Come on. Look at me, and let me do it for you." The young woman's body came alive at the sound of the music. Hands on her waist, torso forward...

"Now we're going to have to move our shoulders. From left to right, always. And hands on hips."

Soon the music took complete possession of the Ethiopian, whose shoulders seemed to dislocate. Her bare feet beat out the rhythm. Kneeling, standing, with a sensual fall of the back, wild shoulders and an arrogant bust, Shoayé was now playing with her hair, moving her head faster and faster. Reine, for her part, was totally captivated by this body, almost in a trance, superb and inhabited. She rose to join her friend in the centre of the room. She released her hair and joined in the dance, albeit a little awkwardly. But Shoayé, with her hands on her friend's shoulders, guided her into the rhythm. They danced for a while, happily savouring this new-found intimacy.

# Ethiopia, Thirteen Months of Sunshine

They landed in the early hours of the morning. The Frenchwoman had not expected to discover such a lively, bustling city, nestling in the heart of green hills. A little dizzy from all the activity, she clung for a moment to her friend's arm. Shoayé was amused by her look of bewilderment.

"The blue and white cars you see everywhere are our taxis."

Reine's eyes were now wide open. The vehicles were popping up all over the place in seemingly total disarray.

"Some of them are a bit... rustic," added Shoayé, laughing. Don't worry, we'll be there soon. You'll soon be able to breathe !

The young woman noticed her friend's use of the familiar form of address for the first time, and it touched her. "But why and where are all these people running ? It's still so early."

Shoayé smiled again : "Let's see, you're in Ethiopia, the land of champions. This is Meskel Square. When we have time, we come and run on the steps you see. Running is the pride of our country. And we excel at it ! So we train whenever we can. We leave football to Brazil and France," she added with a smile. You know, we're here at an altitude of 2,500 metres, which explains the stamina of our athletes. Ethiopia is the land of champions. Don't forget that !

"I didn't know you were so sporty," laughed Reine.

"Not particularly sporty, but terribly Ethiopian ! If you only knew how much I miss my country when I'm in France ! And I want to show you what a beautiful country it is."

They were welcomed by Shoayé's uncle and aunt. Reine was able to visit the school that had left such a lasting impression on her friend. She was charmed by the atmosphere there.

"We're going to go home and rest for a while. Tonight's a party !"

Seeing her friend's surprised expression, Shoaye continued :

"Tomorrow we celebrate the New Year." Reine looked increasingly confused. "It's Meskerem 1, our New Year's Day. Yes, Ethiopia is special, and proud of it. We celebrate our New Year on September 11. Once every four years, our calendar has thirteen months, and to top it all off, here you're more likely to be in the right place at the right time."

At the look of bewilderment on her friend's face, the Ethiopian burst out laughing. "Yes, according to our calendar, you're not 32, but 25. Isn't that wonderful ? Isn't that magic ?" She was now gently mocking her friend.

"If you want to discover our country, you have to let yourself be carried away and accept to put aside your Western reflexes. Come on, tonight it's *injera* and afterwards we'll go dancing. There's a party at school. We're going to have to look our best."

Reine hadn't planned this, and she didn't care. She had brought the bare essentials and had never been much of a dresser. But Shoaye reassured her. Don't worry, she would lend her something.

Shoaye was the star of the evening. She hadn't been home for a long time and hadn't told her friends she was coming back. So it was a reunion party. While Reine rested for a few moments on the school steps, Shoaye joined her, accompanied by a handsome young man.

"This is Alemayehu, my little brother."

"You never told me you had a brother," said Reine, holding out her hand to the young man.

"But I've not told you everything. In fact, I have two brothers, younger than myself. Alemayehu and Mesfin. Alemayehu lives here in Addis. He's a teacher here. Mesfin, the youngest, works with my father."

Reine Pardon looked at young Alemayehu stealthily. She admired his fine features and noticed the small dimple revealed by his charming smile. Wearing dreadlocks, a cap in the colours of Jamaica and a T-shirt bearing the image of Bob Marley, the young man was trying hard to resemble the man who had been nicknamed "The King of Reggae." Nonchalant, even a little haughty, he offered himself up to the gaze of his admirers, of whom there seemed to be many. Reine was struck by the resemblance between brother and sister and, though she couldn't explain it, she was a little disturbed.

The evening ended around three o'clock the next morning. Reine fell into a deep sleep, exhausted by the journey and the unexpected New Year's Eve.

The next day, Mebrat took her friend to the *mercato*. This open-air market was considered to be the biggest in Africa and, like all African markets, it was a veritable enchantment of colours and scents. Reine was lost in this profusion, stunned by so much life. Of course, Alemayehu accompanied them.

*****

Two days later, they packed their bags again. Shoaye first took her to visit Awash, some two hundred kilometres from Addis. The Frenchwoman loved these bush landscapes, far from the high plateaux. She squealed like a child at the crocodiles basking in the sun, motionless and on the lookout, amused by the hippos, marvelling at the zebras and antelopes. It was as if she was entering the heart of the world. She could never forget this emotion. She was back in the landscapes that had made her dream as a child. She thought of her bedside book when she was a little girl. She had dreamt of Africa while reading Joseph Kessel. She thought of little Patricia and her friend King, the marvellous lion, and also of her mother, who had given her this novel for her twelfth birthday ; it had never left her bookshelf. Today, it was there, and she felt as if she recognised everything.

"Lie down on the grass."

Reine Pardon looked at her friend.

"Lie down in the grass and breathe it in. Can you smell it, a bit pungent, a bit bitter ? Let it take hold of you, so you can take it with you. I'd know it anywhere. It's the smell of earth and wind, of the gazelle and the lion, of water and fire, of life and death."

She sat down beside her and, closing her eyes, murmured :

"Listen more often
To things than to beings
The voice of fire is heard
Hear the voice of water
Listen in the wind
The sobbing bush.
It is the breath of the ancestors."

"It's beautiful, isn't it ? It's a poem by Bigaro Diop, a Senegalese poet. I think of these verses when I come here. You're in the heart of the Rift Valley, in the heart of humanity, in the cradle of the world. I've always thought of this region as 'inhabited.' Can't you feel its presence ? They're all here, our ancestors. Our common ancestors.

Reine Pardon smiled, moved.

"Lucy's country...- Back home, we call her Dinqnesh. In Amharic, it means 'You are wonderful.' It's nicer, isn't it ? If you like, we can go to the museum in Addis. I like visiting it. It's a bit of a grandmother. You know, I'm glad you like these landscapes. They belong in part to you, now, too. Don't ever forget them. Tomorrow we leave for the lake, we're expected."

In the middle of the night, Shoayé came to wake her friend. "Get up and follow me. You've got to see this."

They left the caravan they were staying in. The night was blue, the stars bright... A simple crescent, the moon had turned into a smile and lit up the Savannah. A gentle breeze accompanied the two women. The tall grass brushed against their bare legs. They shivered with happiness and pleasure, and also with quietude. The laughter of the hyenas, their astonished cries, a distant roar...

Reine was forever imbued with the magic of that African night and promised herself she would return one day.

***

"Stop here, we'll finish on foot."
The glistening lake, the canoes, the flamingos, the pelicans, the children playing by the water, the women drawing water... nothing had changed since little Shoayé left. Once again, Reine devoured the landscape she with her eyes was discovering, so

different from the one she had just left. Clearly, Ethiopia had many faces. Shoayé grabbed her hand.

"Here we are at my place. Look how beautiful it is !"

The children saw them coming and soon there were a dozen of them following them, laughing. Reine caused a sensation with her white skin and blonde hair. Suddenly, Shoayé stopped. A few metres down the road was her parents' house. In the courtyard, busy sorting coffee beans, was Mebrat. She was sitting on the stoop, in the position that Shoayé knew so well. She wanted to call her mother, but her voice broke. The reunion was simple, full of emotion and modesty. Reine no longer existed. She waited, a little uncomfortable. Mother and daughter seemed unable to tear themselves away from each other.

"Can you introduce me to your friend ?" asked the mother in a lilting language that rattled like so many bubbles. Shoayé turned round with a smile and Reine noticed her misty eyes.

"This is Reine Pardon, whom I've already told you about."

Reine curtsied as she approached. She had heard so much about Mebrat that she felt she knew her, and yet she couldn't help feeling intimidated. Shoayé beamed. Mebrat invited them to drop off their belongings in the cool, dust-free house. Almost the whole village was now gathered at the entrance to their courtyard. They had come to see Shoayé and the *farendje*, the foreigner…

"Where's Dad ?"

Mebrat pointed towards the lake. Yared was pulling his *pirogue* out of the water. He was accompanied by a young man.

"Is that Mesfin ? My goodness, how he's grown !"

"You haven't been back for a long time," smiled her mother."

Just like when she was little, Shoayé dashed off.

"I'm off to meet them !"

Reine chose to stay with Mebrat. She took a few photos of the house, the spectacle of the lake, Mebrat and the children, with their ivory smiles and ebony eyes, who never left the little door, calling out to the photographer with delighted laughter.

The father and daughter soon returned, followed by Mesfin, who had stayed behind. They both looked so happy that Reine chose to immortalise the moment. Yared spoke and his daughter listened respectfully. The surgeon had given way to the former little girl. Of course, her father had aged. The little beard she had always known him for had turned white, as had his hair, and his face had certainly wrinkled, but his smile and his eyes had retained their gentle light. Yared was a good man and it showed. His gnarled body had also aged, and yet he remained strong and vigorous. Reine wanted to photograph the young boy, but he refused. Mebrat, with a slightly embarrassed smile, explained to the young woman that his son was a bit of a loner, a bit of a "savage."

Then Shoayé translated for Reine, who also

smiled and replied that she understood. Then she looked at her daughter :

"Do you know that your father is the new village chief ?"

A few months earlier, the elderly Aklilou had fallen seriously ill. The illness had progressed very rapidly. Shortly before he died, he appointed Yared to replace him. Yared knew how to unite and guide his fellow men, and had had the opportunity to prove it. He had the wisdom of someone who thinks things through, never hesitating to question himself when necessary and, above all, he knew how to listen : an essential quality if you were to be a good, strong and respected leader. Mebrat's voice betrayed all her pride. She leaned her forehead against her husband's shoulder, a fleeting moment of tenderness. Shoayé noticed that her mother had also aged. Her beautiful face had become thinner, and a few wrinkles lit up her eyes. Her tattoo, a small, radiant blue sun adorned her forehead. A black turban covered her hair. Wearing a traditional dress, her only piece of jewellery was a small Coptic cross, the same one Reine had already seen around her daughter's neck. Reine asked for permission to photograph them.

"I'm proud of you, Dad," murmured Shoayé, stroking his hand.

"You should be especially proud of your mother. Where I come from, we say that 'a woman is like a lamp in the house.' Your mother lit up our house and her light lit up the whole village."

He turned to Reine Pardon and bowed. To his daughter's great surprise, he spoke to her in English.

"Since when do you speak English, Dad ?"

"I learned when Aklilou told me he wanted me to succeed him. A village chief has to be modern, doesn't he ? And you know your mother... She wanted to learn too. Welcome to our village," he continued, "you are going to attend a great ceremony. You'll be the only *farendje*. Above all, always ask before taking photographs. Some of our people believe that the soul lies in the eyes and that a photograph could steal it from them."

Reine remembered a photo of a priest she'd seen at Mebrat's house. He was indeed looking away, clearly uncomfortable. She promised.

"What ceremony are you talking about ?"

"A grand ceremony. The first of its kind. But I won't tell you any more than that, except that you'll be happy, and so will your friend." Yared's tone was solemn.

"Genet is by the lake. Go and join, her Shoayé. I think she's waiting for you. Stay with us, Reine, and I'll show you around the village..."

The reunion between the two sisters was like a meeting of the minds. They were only three years apart, yet Genet seemed older and more tired. Six successive pregnancies had taken their toll on her. Genet was bringing up four girls and two boys. Between the coffee she harvested, the chores of fetching wood and water from the lake and the housework, hers was a hard life. The two sisters talked endlessly. Genet talked about picking coffee, she talked about her husband. What about her, Shoayé ? Did she have someone in her life, a man to accompany her and cherish her ? Shoayé, as always, evaded the question with a wave of her hand. She didn't have the time. Perhaps later.

They talked about their childhood, the jealousy of the eldest, the loneliness of the youngest, her departure and loss. Then their discussion became more intimate. Genet needed advice. Could Shoayé help her stop having children ? She had suffered so much at the birth of her last... She had almost died. She was convinced that another birth would kill her. Shoayé offered to examine her in Addis. Genet agreed.

# The Truth, and the Morning, Brighten with Time

It was still very early in the morning and yet there was already a huge crowd on the lakeside path. People had come from far and wide to attend the event. The women were laughing loudly, some were singing, impatient and curious too, while others were chatting, all in the joy of their reunion. Under the big tree stood Yared, soon to be joined by the men of the village. They waited, smoking or chewing *khat*. The reason everyone had gathered together on this special day was that Tsehaye, who no longer excised, had decided – albeit symbolically – to hand in her razor blade. Although Tsehaye had not practised for a long time, she was still the reference in the region and was still asked to train other young women. Her decision would certainly be commented on, and perhaps one day emulated. And above all, after this ceremony, Tsehaye would no longer be the one who excised, but the one who had had the wisdom to hand over her blade. The elderly woman didn't know how old she was, but she felt that life was leaving her, little

by little. Soon, she would have to give an account...
She dreaded this day and longed more than anything to go in peace.

When everyone arrived, Yared motioned for
them to sit down and asked Mebrat, Shoayé, Reine
and Genet to join him. There was silence. The ten-
sion was palpable. Everyone waited.

The old woman arrived at last, walking slowly,
aware of the stares she was receiving. She greeted Yared respectfully and made her way towards
Mebrat, Shoayé and Reine. As for Genet, she preferred to remain in the crowd.

It was to her daughter-in-law that the old woman
handed, wrapped in a cloth, the old razor blade.
Mebrat was touched by this gesture and took it
gently before handing it to Yared, before whom
Tsehaye bowed. Yared rose to his feet, and he
moved towards the now former cutter to help her
to her feet, assuring her of his respect as a leader,
but also as her son. She had no business bowing like
that, he whispered. Then he urged her to use her
knowledge of plants to help the community. It was
a long walk to the dispensary, so she was needed in
the village. And who knows, maybe she could train a
few young people. Yes, her knowledge was needed.

The ceremony ended with songs. Everyone ate
the food that the women had brought, taking
advantage of the moment to get together and talk.
Reine Pardon took photos and was finally able to
meet Tsehaye.

Her face was wrinkled like an old fruit. Her hair

was whitened by the years, her smile rare and toothless, it was difficult to give her an age ; perhaps eighty... A cataract had whitened her left eye and had already stolen her right. Her hands trembled as she held the stick she was leaning on. Reine couldn't take her eyes off them. It seemed to her that she could hear the screams of all the girls whom those hands had hurt. It was a strange feeling, a mixture of fascination, curiosity and she had to admit to herself repugnance too. Tsehaye represented tradition. She was a woman who was both the victim and the executioner, even if it was "in spite of herself."

The journalist was keen to meet the old woman. It was important for her to hear her testimony. She needed to get to know her to finally understand.

"Don't judge me."

The journalist was startled and looked at the old woman who was staring at her with white eyes.

"I'm not judging you." Reine had the feeling that the old woman was reading her...

"I know who you are. What I'd like to know is, why have you come ?"

"I've come because I'm going to write a book about Mebrat."

"So that's it... And are you going to talk about me ?" The journalist admitted that yes, she would be talking about Tsehaye.

"Well, in that case, let me tell you about it." Tsehaye opened up, encouraged by the solemnity of the ceremony. Yes, of course, other women would continue to cut, she was aware of that – you don't abandon a tradition so easily – but she, Tsehaye, would remain the one who had set the example. After all, she too had had to defy centuries of belief. She should not be forgotten. At last, people would no longer shudder when they saw her, or avoid her house. So she confided in the journalist her solitude, her nights haunted by the cries of the children she had mutilated. She also recounted the weight of the enmity that had grown over the years, a mixture of fear and respect, the glances heavy with reproach. The nicknames too...

Mebrat had joined them. For a long time, she had blamed Tsehaye for her rejection of the ritual, but now she realised the extent to which her mother-in-law had also been a victim of tradition.

The old woman agreed to have her photo taken with her daughter-in-law. Soon they were joined by Shoayé and Genet. Three generations of women separated by tradition were finally reunited. This photo was one of victory. The old woman also asked to speak to Sennait. Of course, this was painful. The two women had always done everything to avoid each other since the tragedy. But so many years later, the time had come to accept Tsehaye's apology. Sennait had understood, the cutter was not really responsible. Of course, it was her blade that had killed her little Moulou... But Tsehaye was obeying a tradition stronger than herself, just as Sennait had done by accepting the ritual.

Mebrat freed me, added the old woman. Oh,

of course, I didn't understand it straight away. I was angry with her for upsetting everything. I was afraid of this new society that was being born, because I knew that Mebrat would be joined by other mothers. What was to become of me ? What use would I be now ? But now it's not the same, and I've made peace with myself. When the time comes, I'm ready to join little Moulou and the other victims. Yes, because I've finally understood that they weren't my victims, but those of tradition. Yes, I'm going to be able to sleep at last.

Against all odds, Tsehaye became Mebrat's ally. Together, they would be stronger, the former cutter, the first "resistance fighter," mother-in-law and daughter-in-law reunited at last. The symbolism was powerful.

The two young women left the village two days later. Genet accompanied them to Addis Ababa. As agreed, Shoayé examined her. What she saw shocked her. While she examined her, she talked to her about the different methods of contraception she could offer her, and then, with great gentleness and simple words, she explained that she could help her with reconstructive surgery. Oh sure, she wouldn't be able to rebuild everything, but at least it would give her lasting relief. She explained the surgical procedure, the pain that would fade, the sensations she might discover. Genet hesitated, very embarrassed, but finally agreed. They agreed on a date. The operation would take place in France, and Genet would ask Mebrat to accompany her.

***

The number of public ceremonies during which female cutters handed over their equipment to the village chief increased. Of course, little girls were still being circumcised, but the number of interventions was clearly on the rise. Those who had escaped the ritual were no longer stigmatised. Their eldest daughters found husbands, which reassured the mothers who were still hesitating.

As planned, Mebrat and Genet came to France and Shoayé was able to operate on her sister. The operation, although delicate, was conclusive. The day after the operation, Reine Pardon came to take a photo of the two sisters, two united and smiling sisters. What a long way they had come since their childhood on the shores of the great lake ! A few days later, it was Mebrat's turn to decide. She had hesitated. Shoayé was her daughter, it was not a simple situation. They discussed it at length. Shoayé found the right words. Mebrat had spared her, now it was her turn to do something for her. Mebrat had chosen not to say anything to Yared. It was her decision, the conclusion of her commitment. More than ever, she felt alive.

It was like a liberation for Mebrat. She had become the woman she had always dreamed of being. She felt she had won a victory, and she was proud of it.

Mebrat and Genet stayed with Shoaye for a few weeks. The three women talked, confided in each other and rediscovered each other. There was so much catching up to do. Genet asked her sister to forgive her for what she had done to her as a child. But all that was long gone. When they left, they were transformed, more serene, more fulfilled. Both were impatient to be reunited with their loved ones. Mebrat especially : what would Yared, her long-time partner, say ? He had always been there, by her side, strong and faithful. She couldn't wait to join him in the privacy of their little home.

***

A year later, Reine Pardon and Shoayé were back on the shores of the lake. A party was organised in their honour, with the whole village in attendance and Alemayehu taking part in the evening. Reine had brought the photos she had taken at the ceremony a year earlier. Together, everyone looked at them and, of course, commented on them. The village, Mebrat sorting coffee, Yared on his *pirogue*, Genet and her sister... One photo caused a sensation : Tsehaye handing her blade to Mebrat. Tsehaye, now blind, was accompanied by a little girl, an orphan she had taken in. The little girl guided her while the old woman taught her about plants. They got on well together, and Tsehaye, at last, was able to enjoy her old age, free of her old ways, from the yoke of a custom that had separated her from her family for so many years. She was now a loving grandmother and a respected woman. At the sight of this last photograph, the village applauded. Shoayé and Genet helped their grandmother to her feet, joined by Mebrat... These four women had become the symbol of women who fight and win.

Finally, the family left for Addis Ababa. It was at Mebrat's House that Reine decided to present her book. It was Mebrat who had chosen the title... *The Flowers of the lake*. With Mebrat's agreement, she chose to dedicate it to Mebrat, Shoayé, Genet and also... Tsehaye. They had planned to immortalise the moment in the living room of Mebrat's House, where a large section of the wall read : "Flowers are not meant to be cut."

# Thanks

I would like to express my gratitude to Mr Asmamaw Kelemu, doctor in economics and politics, for his help. His information was invaluable.

Thanks to his niece, my friend Giulia Malgheri, for her availability and patience, and to Dalia Mesloub and Géraldine Dewez for their unconditional support.

All of this work was possible thanks to the GAMS National Federation (Group for the Abolition of Sexual Mutilation), whose advice helped me to embark on this new adventure.

My special thoughts go to Dr Denis Mukwege, repair surgeon and Nobel Peace Prize winner, dedicated to the cause of women.

Finally, I'd like to extend a warm hug to Philippe Morel, who kindly entrusted me with one of his sculptures. Thanks to him, my heroines now have a face.

# By the same author

*De Vous à Moi*, La Rémanence, (testimony)

*Mémoire de Babouchka*, La Rémanence (life story, ghostwriting)

*Les Fleurs du lac*, La Rémanence (novel)

*Le cabanon jaune*, La Rémanence (novel)

*Une lumière dans la nuit*, La Rémanence (life story)

*La fugue de Julie Anne*, In Octavo Editions (novel)

*L'harmonica le trombone et le parapuie*, In Octavo

*D'encre et de pierre*, La Rémanence (collection of short stories and poems)

*Moonlight Serenade over the channel*, BOD

# Table des matières


Preface...................15
Eyes Mother...................23
The Seventh Day...................43
Say No Even When It Is Not Convenient...............51
Standing Firm Against All Odds...................59
Mebrat's House...................71
Understanding to Fight Better...................79
Ethiopia, Thirteen Months of Sunshine...............93
The Truth, and the Morning, Brighten with Time....105
Thanks...................113
By the same author...................115

Publisher : BoD · Books on Demand,
31 avenue Saint-Rémy, 57600 Forbach, bod@bod.fr
Print : Libri Plureos GmbH,
Friedensallee 273, 22763 Hamburg (Allemagne)
Dépôt légal : Juin 2025